Things Will Get Better

by Janet Reed • illustrated by Cindy Clark

Chapters

Harcourt

Orlando   Boston   Dallas   Chicago   San Diego

Visit *The Learning Site!*

www.harcourtschool.com

Shelter

Sue Murphy lived with her father and her brother, Ben. Her mother had died when she was a baby, so Sue had never known her. Sue was ten now, and Ben was seventeen, almost grown up. Sue's family lived in a small town in Ohio. She went to a school nearby and was one of the best students there.

The stock market crash in October 1929 marked the beginning of the Great Depression. The Murphys, like millions of other families in the United States, suffered. By the summer of 1930, factories in their town had been forced to close. The people who owned them no longer had enough money to pay their employees. Sue's father and brother both lost their jobs. After that, the banks closed, and Mr. Murphy lost his savings. The bills kept arriving, but he couldn't pay them. The Murphys weren't sure what they should do.

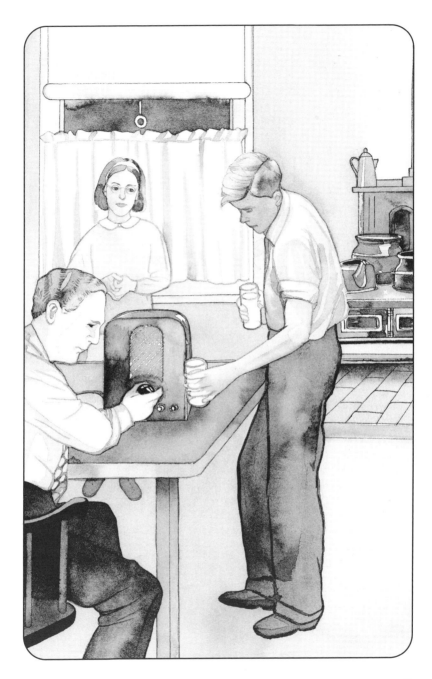

The years between 1929 and 1940 were hard for everyone. In these years of the Great Depression many people were without jobs.

Times were hard. The people who lost their jobs were not lazy. They wanted to work. There were very few jobs. No work meant no money.

When people heard that there was a job offered, they would rush to get it. Often they stood in line for hours, hoping to get work.

Time after time, there was no work for them.

One night at dinner, the Murphys had a serious talk. There were no jobs in town, but Mr. Murphy had heard there might be some in Pennsylvania. He had decided that he and Ben should go there.

"Sue, I want you to stay in school here. We have no money except for a small amount that Ben and I will need for food."

"Then where will I stay until you find work and can send for me?" Sue asked glumly.

"I've spoken to the Greys," Mr. Murphy assured her. "They have agreed to have you stay with them for the school year."

In the autumn of 1930, Sue went to stay with her friend Alice Grey's family while her father and brother went to Pennsylvania to look for work.

Mr. Murphy and Ben took Sue to Alice's house. Mrs. Grey, Alice, and her sister Meg greeted Sue warmly. Soon it was time for Sue to say good-bye to her father and brother. They both hugged Sue tightly. She tried not to cry.

Alice's grandmother, Mrs. Jones, who was Mrs. Grey's mother, also lived with the family. Mrs. Jones stayed in the kitchen when Sue arrived. "I don't know why I agreed to have a stranger living here," she thought. "This girl isn't family." Fortunately, she kept her thoughts to herself.

Whenever Sue was around, however, Mrs. Jones gave her the silent treatment. Often she even left the room.

Friends and Enemies

Alice thought it was great fun to have Sue live with her family. She and Sue had been best friends since first grade, so they shared many interests and pastimes. They both enjoyed ice skating, drawing, and singing, but their real passion was the movies.

Sometimes, when Mrs. Grey had enough money, they went to Saturday matinees. It cost each of them a dime to go. Sometimes they saw two films, a newsreel, and a cartoon. For hours afterward, they would discuss which movie star they liked best. They decorated the room they shared with pictures of movie stars cut from old movie magazines. The girls never had any reason to bicker.

As the weeks passed, Mrs. Jones's attitude toward Sue seemed to worsen. Often Sue would ask, "Mrs. Jones, may I help you in the kitchen?"

Every time, Mrs. Jones answered irritably, "No, Miss Murphy, you're a guest. My grandchildren will help if I need it."

Mrs. Jones always called Sue "Miss Murphy," as if Sue had better keep her bags packed because she wasn't there to stay. Understandably, Sue was quite uncomfortable around Mrs. Jones.

Mrs. Grey watched this with concern. Her mother had never been that rude to anyone. Mrs. Grey was at a loss to explain her mother's behavior, but she didn't like to see her mother speak unkindly to Sue. Mrs. Grey finally decided it was time to have a talk.

"Mother, why do you have a grudge against Sue?" Mrs. Grey asked. "What has she done to annoy you?"

At first, Mrs. Jones didn't answer, but then she said, "The child is nothing to me. She's a stranger in my home."

"Sue is Alice's friend. The only one who still thinks of Sue as a stranger is you. These are difficult times," Mrs. Grey continued. "Can't you try a little bit harder?"

"I'm sorry, but we should never have agreed to let her live in this house!"

"Sue's been kind and helpful. She has a friendly disposition. She even acts as a tutor for Meg in arithmetic," Mrs. Grey pointed out.

"I can't help how I feel. I just do not trust her," Mrs. Jones said.

Sometimes when Sue was alone, she would become very sad because she missed her father and her brother. "I wish times would get better so we could be together again," she thought.

Sue knew her father and brother were not having an easy time either. There weren't enough jobs to go around. Mr. Murphy sent money to the Greys when he could, but most of the time he just sent a letter. Sue knew her father and brother didn't have enough money to send for her yet.

Sue realized she wasn't the only one having a hard time. Many of her friends' fathers had lost their jobs and left for other states to find work. Hers was not the only family that had needed to separate for a while. Sue knew she was lucky that the Greys — at least most of them — had welcomed her into their home.

Sue was grateful for her friendly relationships with Alice, Meg, and Mrs. Grey. However, she still wished that Mrs. Jones liked her more.

 # After the Storm

In December of 1930, there was a great blizzard in Ohio. All activity in the community froze. Even the trolley cars were stopped by drifts of snow that were taller than a person.

The snow was so deep that when people went out, they couldn't see where the sidewalks were. Some cars were buried in snow.

All the schools were closed, so Meg, Alice, and Sue stayed home. The girls tried to make a tunnel in the snow, but the snow was too hard and too cold. They made snow people instead and dressed them in old hats and scarves.

At supper the three girls were very tired but very happy — that is, until Mrs. Jones came storming into the room. She was furious.

"Miss Murphy, I'm missing fifty cents, and I would like to know where it is."

Sue was stunned. "I don't know. I . . . I didn't take it," she stuttered.

"Well, if you didn't, I don't know who did!"

"Sue," Mrs. Grey said quietly, "go up to your room, please. I'll be up in a moment." Sue left the table without another word.

"Mother, are you sure?" asked Mrs. Grey.

"Of course, I'm sure! The money was right on top of my chest of drawers, and now it's gone."

Mrs. Grey found Sue crying in the room that she and Alice shared.

"Oh, Mrs. Grey," Sue wailed, "I didn't do it. I'd never do that." Tears streamed down her face. "I never even go into her room."

"I believe you, Sue. My mother can be a little hard on people sometimes. Don't worry."

"It's so unfair. I know she doesn't want me here, but I would never steal. Will you make me leave?"

"Now don't be silly. You're more than welcome here. These are hard times, and we have to stick together. Things will get better."

Sue nodded and wiped her tears away.

On the Saturday morning after the blizzard, Mrs. Jones set out for the corner grocery store. On her way down a steep hill, she slipped and fell on the icy ground.

Mrs. Jones realized she had sprained her ankle. She tried to get up and couldn't. She called out, but no one heard her. It was still extremely cold, and there was no one around to help her. She rubbed her hands together to try to stay warm.

Then Mrs. Jones tried to get up again and couldn't. The pain in her ankle made her feel faint. She almost cried, but she didn't because she realized it wouldn't do any good. She closed her eyes and hoped for a miracle.

Suddenly she felt two small hands pulling her upright. She opened her eyes and found herself sitting up in the snow.

"I'll help you get up, Mrs. Jones. You can lean on me. I'm pretty strong, so don't be afraid."

It was Sue Murphy! Mrs. Jones was too shaky to speak. She leaned on the girl she had called a thief. Sue now was Mrs. Jones's rescuer, taking her home.

Mrs. Jones looked at Sue and said, "Thank you, Miss Murphy." This time she said the name differently, with gratitude.

"Oh . . . You're welcome, Ma'am."

Then Mrs. Jones plunged her cold hands deep into her pockets. Suddenly she looked stricken. "Oh, my! Oh, no." She removed her right hand from her coat pocket and opened it. In her palm lay her two missing quarters. She said, "Oh, my! I have been so unfair to you. I'm very sorry for the horrible way I treated you. Can you forgive such a silly woman?"

Sue nodded and smiled warmly at Mrs. Jones.

Mrs. Jones held out the two quarters and placed them in Sue's hand. "I want you to have these. Please accept them and my promise to treat you fairly. That is what you deserve."

15

Sue looked at the coins in her hand. "Thank you, Mrs. Jones."

"Spend the money on those movie magazines you and Alice like so much!" Mrs. Jones added.

When Sue and Mrs. Jones arrived back home, a letter had arrived for Sue. It was from her father, explaining that he and Ben had both found work! They would send for her as soon as they had located a suitable place to live.

Sue never spent the two quarters on movies or magazines. To this day, she has those quarters in a little box. On the box are the words, "Things will get better."

Think and Respond

1. Why does the author provide information about the Great Depression in the first chapter?

2. Compare and contrast the attitudes of Mrs. Grey and Mrs. Jones toward Sue.

3. What is the theme of this story?

4. How do you know that Mrs. Jones is a stubborn person who is fixed in her ways?

5. How did Sue's life at the Greys' home differ from life with her own family? How was it similar?

6. Imagine that your best friend came to live with your family for a year. In one column, write the advantages of such an arrangement. In the second column, write the challenges.

 The Great Depression During the Depression, the Civilian Conservation Corps (CCC) helped the environment. Find out about the CCC. What did it do to help your town or state? Write a newspaper article about its activities and share it with your classmates.

 School-Home Connection Interview a relative or someone in your community who experienced the Great Depression. What effect did it have on his or her life? Compare and contrast this with Sue's experience.

Level

ISBN 0-15-323262-5

9 780153 232626